The Fish that Talked

Retold by Rosie Dickins

Illustrated by
Graham Philpot

Reading Consultant: Alison Kelly
Roehampton University

Long ago, in India, there was a young man named Manu.

One day, Manu was
wading in a stream.

A tiny fish swam into
his hands.

The fish sparkled with a
silvery light.

"Help!" it said. "The big fish want to eat me."

It talks!

"Poor little thing,"
said Manu.

He cupped his
hands and carried
the fish home.

He put the fish into a jar
of water...

Splash!

and fed it with crumbs.

10

It grew...

and grew...

I have no
room to swim.

until it was too
big for the jar.

11

So Manu took the fish to the well...

Splash!

and fed it with bread.

It grew and grew...

until it was too
big for the well.

13

So Manu carried the fish
to the river.

Splash!

He didn't feed
it, but...

15

"Please take me to the sea," begged the fish.

Manu groaned. "He'll weigh a ton," he thought.

This is magic.

But amazingly, the fish
was as light as air.

Manu walked to the
seashore and threw the
fish into the sea.

"Thank you," said the fish.

You are a good man.

"Now it's my turn to help you."

"There is going to be a great flood."

"You must build a boat to save all living things."

So Manu built a
huge boat...

and filled it with plants
and animals.

Soon, dark clouds
filled the sky.

Then, the rain came.

27

It rained and rained, until
water covered the land.

Only Manu's boat floated
above the waves.

The wind howled and
waves crashed around
the boat.

"We must find shelter,"
said Manu, "or we'll sink!"

He peered into the dark...
and saw a silvery light.

It was the talking fish.

Throw me
a rope.

The fish pulled the boat through the storm. After a long, long time, they reached a great mountain.

We'll be safe now.

Its top rose out of the
flood like an island.

Suddenly, the fish changed...

"I am Brahma,* lord of all creatures," it said.

* Say **Braa**-*muh*

Manu gasped. Brahma
was a powerful god.

"I have saved you so you can rebuild the world."

"And you, Manu, will be its king."

"Rule wisely!"
said Brahma.

"I will," promised Manu.

Brahma vanished in a
flash of silvery light.

Manu never saw Brahma
again. But he never forgot
what the god said.

After the flood, he worked
hard to rebuild the world.

And he ruled wisely and
well for the rest of his days.

About this story

The Fish that Talked comes from
an ancient Indian poem called
The Mahabharata,* which tells
of gods and men and war. The
original poem is 18 books long
and over 2,000 years old.

In some versions, it is the Hindu
god Vishnu who takes the form
of the fish that grew and grew
and saved the world.

* Say *Muh-har-**bar**-uh-tuh*

Indian story consultant: Arshia Sattar
Series editor: Lesley Sims
Designed by Maria Pearson
Digital manipulation by Louise Flutter

First published in 2008 by Usborne Publishing Ltd., Usborne House,
83-85 Saffron Hill, London EC1N 8RT, England. www.usborne.com
Copyright © 2008 Usborne Publishing Ltd.

All rights reserved. No part of this publication may be reproduced,
stored in a retrieval system or transmitted in any form or by any
means, electronic, mechanical, photocopying, recording or otherwise,
without the prior permission of the publisher. The name Usborne
and the devices ♀ ☻ are Trade Marks of Usborne Publishing Ltd.
Printed in China. UE. First published in America in 2008.